A BAKER GOT ME

RYAN

JUST BAE

ISBN: 978-1-925988-54-3

CONTENTS

CHAPTER ONE

"Ryan! Can you start closing up, please?" calls his mother from the washroom, her voice nearly drowned out by the whirring of the dishwasher. Ryan wipes his hands on the tea towel tucked into his apron, leaving streaks of turquoise royal icing on the fraying cotton and heads towards the door.

He adjusts his chef's cap as he steps onto the shop floor, noting the time on the register reads 5:25 pm, just five minutes until closing. In front of a busy display of ribbons, candles and decorations, is a woman in her thirties with dark curly hair styled into loose curls over her shoulders. She has on a forest green, knee-length dress, with a black jacket, and a pair of black and white Adidas trainers. In one hand is a black laptop bag, and on her opposite shoulder is what Ryan recognizes as a Louie Vuitton handbag.

The woman reaches out to slip a large number one candle off its hook, adjusting her laptop bag, and holding it in the same hand. She fingers the variety of spools carefully, feeling the weight and texture of the ribbons, considering what she wants. Once the woman decides on a yellow and white checkered one she turns, only to freeze in surprise at the sight of Ryan. Their eyes meet, both not expecting to be confronted by such beauty on this quiet Monday afternoon.

"Hi," Ryan says smiling, having quickly straightening himself. "Can I help you with that?"

"Oh, yes," the woman says, looking

equally as if she's had to snap herself back to reality. She points down to a ribbon she just decided on. "May I please have a meter of this?"

"Sure," Ryan says, grabbing the scissors from the pot next to the register and walking over to measure and cut the length. He rolls it up before asking if that's all. The woman explains she needs to get a few more things, so Ryan offers to watch the candle and ribbon by the register, as well as her laptop bag. "I'm about to lock the door," Ryan says, pointing to the clock which now reads 5:29. "No one will run off with it, and if I run off with it, at least you know where I work?"

The woman giggles at his lame joke, and it makes Ryan's heart stutter.

The sound reminds Ryan of the clatter of fridge-cold chocolate chips being poured into a bowl of cookie dough; a sound he's loved since childhood when he and his grandmother used to bake together, him standing on a chair at her kitchen counters, wearing an apron. Ryan always used to 'accidentally' tip one or two of the chocolate pieces onto the surface instead of the bowl, and he and his grandmother decided they weren't destined for the cookies and should be eaten there and then. It was a sound of joy and happiness.

But then the woman frowns, "I'm sorry. Am I stopping you from closing up? I can just pay and go." She says it sincerely, though he can tell she is eager to buy more.

"No, no, it's fine," Ryan says smiling, walking towards the door and turning the key in the lock at the bottom - in the most un-menacing way he can, trying to make it clear that she can leave any time and he's not trapping her into his cake shop to have his way with her . . . though his pants tighten just a smidge when he considers it. Ryan clears his throat. "We have plenty of cleaning up to do here, take your time."

"Thanks," she says and places the candle and her bag on the counter before taking a small wicker basket from a stack on the floor and wandering towards the rows of colored fondants. She picks up a packet of grey modeling paste, pausing to read the label 'Miller's Cake Shop' logo on it. "Is this homemade?" the woman asks.

"Yeah," Ryan says. "Pretty much everything in this shop is. All organic, no artificial sweeteners or preservatives."

"That's great," the woman says. "My sister-in-law will love that."

"Are you making a cake for her?"

"Yeah. Well, it's for my niece. She turns one in a week and we're having a party this weekend."

"How lovely," Ryan smiles. "First birthdays are always the best. Well, I'll leave you, got some frosting I need to put in the fridge. Just shout when you're ready or if you need any help."

"Okay, thanks."

Ryan returns to the kitchen and leans against the counter for a minute. Then, he puts the frostings into containers and affixes the appropriate labels before placing them in the fridge. Ryan notes down the temperatures into the logbook, before moving on to check the stocks of butter, eggs, and fruit, deciding whether he needs to put an order in tonight or tomorrow. He tries not to let his mind wander back out onto the shop floor, where the impossibly beautiful woman is currently browsing through the racks of cutters, molds, sprinkles and other decorations.

When he's finished and has wiped down the last of the surfaces, Ryan hears the soft clearing of a throat. He takes off his hat and white apron – now stained from a day of piping mermaid cupcakes and tempering chocolate – and throws them into the corner. The woman smiles waiting for him by the till, carrying a wicker basket full of cake tin, a rolling pin, parchment paper, sprinkles, candles, and ribbons. The woman seems to be buying literally everything she needs to make a birthday cake.

"Can I get a board and a box too?" the woman asks, gesturing to the neatly stacked white ones and silver boards behind him. After selecting the size for her tin, Ryan unpacks the basket onto the counter and offers for her to purchase one of their jute bags to take it all home in.

"I love the branding," the woman says, tracing the shape of their logo where it's been printed onto the bag. "Vibrant colors, and crispy design. Eye-catching. Very simple and effective."

"Thanks," Ryan says. "I designed it."

"You did?"

"Yeah."

"I'm impressed," the woman says, her voice drops a little and her eyes flick up to meet his. He slows his ringing-up of her items, electricity sparking between them for a fraction of a second before she averts her eyes and he clears his throat, trying to dispel the awkwardness.

In an attempt to fill the silence, Ryan asks her about the things she's buying, and she admits to never having made a cake before. He comments that with the amount it's going to cost her she should have asked him to make the cake for her instead.

"Could you?"

"Sorry," Ryan says, scratching behind his ear.

"We're fully booked for wedding season."

The woman hums and explains that's how she ended up in this predicament. After Ryan offers her a questioning glance, she explains. Turns out, the friend of her sister-in-law who was originally supposed to make the cake broke her arm. Too late to order one from the bakery nearby, and with their kitchen being a disaster zone due to renovations, they were left with no other option but to accept her offer to do it. The family friends' eldest brother nor his wife could, as they're flying in from Boston for the weekend, neither can her sister or mother because they're in Europe until Thursday.

The woman rests her elbows on the counter and lowers her head into her hands. "I really don't know why they agreed, or why I even offered. I think no cake would have been a better option!"

"Hey now, I'm sure you can do it," Ryan says. "If you need any tips this week just come on in, I'd be happy to help."

"Thanks."

"Where is your mom and sister traveling in Europe?" Ryan asks, interested, having spent a year of his early twenties backpacking around Europe and trying to gain apprenticeships in bakeries, first in France, then Switzerland, before finding he really couldn't crack the code and ended up in Yorkshire, somehow managing to set up a place at Dolly's Tea Parlor in Brantham.

"They were in France first, but they've been at Wimbledon for a couple of weeks now."

"Cool. For tennis?" Ryan said.

"Not now," the woman said looking at her feet. "My sister was a player before."

"Your sister was playing?" Ryan said. "At Wimbledon?"

"Yeah, Jessica Roth. Have you heard of her?"

"You mean, three-time Grand Slam winner, two-time Olympic medalist, and sweetheart Jessie Roth is your sister?"

"Yeah," she sighs. "She's the one."

"I thought she retired?" Ryan said.

"She and Roger got a wildcard into the mixed doubles," she shrugs.

"Roger…?"

"The Roger," the woman mumbles, looking down at her wallet before retrieving her credit card and holding out for him to take.

Ryan gapes but quickly snaps his mouth shut seeing the woman's look of mild exasperation. He finishes ringing up her items and tries not to grimace at the $75 everything comes to. Glancing up to see that she's looking down in her bag, Ryan turns the display on the register away, so she cannot see the total. "That'll be $50 please."

He thinks for a moment that the woman might be onto him, her eyes narrowing. Ryan takes her credit card and inserts it into the reader, waiting for it to connect.

"Sorry," he says, as the device takes its sweet old time to ask her for her pin number.

"No problem," she says. "These machines are often pains."

"No, I meant, I'm sorry about the thing with your sister. I know what it's like to have an older sibling who everyone has heard of." Ryan shrugs when she looks up. The woman's eyes glance on the logo on the wall behind Ryan, possibly to the framed picture of the replica Hawks jersey cake he made with 'DALE 22' on the back.

"Oh," she says. "Grayson Miller, he's your brother?"

"Yes."

"I mean—at least we get good tickets?" she says.

"I can get box seats at the Bellevue whenever," Ryan says.

"But no good when they're on the other side of the world and you have a court date?"

"Yeah not much good when they're for a match that finishes at 11pm and you have to be up at 4am to bake," Ryan says.

They look at each other suspended in the moment. "Well," the woman says, as she keys in her pin. "I best be off and let you get on with your evening. Thanks for everything—" She scans his embroidered name on his white chef's jacket—Ryan.

"You're welcome. By the way, what's your name?"

"Trina."

"I'm—"

"Ryan. I know," Trina says pointing to his name tag.

Ryan chuckles while Trina unlocks the shop door letting herself out, and raising her hand goodbye.

CHAPTER TWO

Trina nearly falls on her face as she enters the cake shop on her lunch break, a strong wind that's picked up pushes the door open harder than she was ready for and pulling her in. Her black heels slide underneath her.

"Hey there," Ryan says comes out of nowhere, as does his arm, wrapping around her waist. Trina recovers herself quickly and moves away as soon as she can. The ghost of his toned forearm against her sends a shiver up her spine.

"Hello again," he says. An errant curl

has fallen onto Ryan's forehead and Trina can't take her eyes off it, doing everything in her power not to lick her lips at the man she spent the rest of yesterday evening trying to get out of her head.

"Hi." Trina's hand comes up to her face to tug a strand of hair from her lips, which she had coated with lip balm before leaving the office minutes ago. As she tucks the final tendril behind her ear, Trina realizes that the shop is silent and that Ryan's watching her intently.

A car horn sounds outside and Ryan's eyes snap back to reality. "How's your cake coming along?"

"Oh. Not well," Trina huffs, fixing her handbag and removing the lanyard from around her neck, fiddling with the clip.

"Oh no," Ryan says. "What happened?"

Trina shrugs her shoulders and waves her hands. "I have no idea, but what came out of the oven couldn't be called a cake!" Ryan raises his eyebrows. "I think the measurements were off or something? Whatever it was, the whole thing was a waste of time."

Ryan grimaces.

"I remember seeing something I liked yesterday. Can you show me where your cake mix is?" Trina chuckles.

"Of course! Follow me." Ryan waves his hand to follow him to the wooden shelves stacked with multiple brown bags with orange 'Miller's Cake Shop' labels.

"You make this yourself, too?"

"Yeah," Ryan says. "All blended by yours truly. All-natural, all organic. Just add liquid; Hell! you can even make them vegan."

"Wow!" Trina looks over them, her mouth waters as she reads all the flavors. "These all look delicious, I don't know what to choose."

"Would you like to try one?"

"Huh—sure why not," Trina says slurring. "But as long as it's not too much trouble? I don't want to eat anyone's cake."

"No worries."

Ryan heads over to the table in the corner with three spindly chairs arranged around it and Trina follows him. She puts her bag on one of the others and sets her lanyard down. She notices Ryan glance at it, and Trina is glad that she'd made her hair for the day.

"What does the 'T' stand for?" he asks.

"Oh, it's just my name," she says thinking she heard Ryan whisper something under his breath.

"Pardon?" she asks.

Ryan shakes his head. "Nothing, just cake!" He says. "You don't have any allergies, do you?" She shakes her head 'No.' "Great, I'll be back, Trinnie." Ryan dashes off and she can't help but smile hearing his giddiness.

Ryan returns from the kitchen carrying

a white cake stand and places it on the table. He takes a seat across from her and Trina switches her attention to it, having spent the time he was gone admiring the interior design of the shop; a pleasant aesthetic of white walls and dark wood, with touches of orange, black, and brass in the furnishings, artwork and light fixings.

"Wow," Trina says, looking at the cake in front of her. It was cut into eight slices, and instead of being one flavor, each was different.

Ryan turns the stand as he points:

"So, this slice is lemon zest and fresh raspberry with raspberry coulis-rippled buttercream.

The second is lemon mousse with lemon buttercream and shavings of white chocolate.

The third is Madagascan vanilla topped with whipped cream and seasonal berries.

The fourth is three-shade vanilla with vanilla buttercream.

The fifth is a dark chocolate chip with orange zest buttercream.

The sixth is red velvet with cream cheese frosting.

The seventh is carrot with orange zest cream cheese frosting.

And the last is a rich and moist chocolate with dark chocolate ganache."

Trina can feel her mouth-watering at the prospect of frosting all of them. She's glad she didn't pick up her usual chicken and avocado wrap on her way here; a little cake won't hurt for lunch, particularly on a week like this, right? She looks back up at him, hoping there's no drool on her shirt.

"Wow," Trina says again. "These look so delicious!"

Ryan passes her a cake fork and a heavy napkin. "Dig in," he says as he turns the cake plate around so the raspberry slice is the one directly in front of her. "I recommend you start with the lightest and then work your way around to the dark chocolate one, I think you can enjoy the textures and flavors better. Oh, and you'll want to cleanse the plate between each." Ryan jumps up and grabs a carafe of water and a couple of glasses from behind the register, causing the table to wobble as he sits in haste. Trina glances in amusement as he turns the cake stand around and lifts the first slice down onto a small plate in the stack he brought over earlier.

Trina digs in, glad to see that he's also holding a fork and is joining her, making her feel a lot less guilty about this extravagance. The flavors explode on her tongue, the hint of lemon pairing perfectly with the tang of the raspberries, the gentle sweetness of buttercream balancing beautifully. Trina could easily devour the whole slice, but she'd never been able to manage the others, so instead, she reaches for the glass of water, takes a sip and then moves onto the next one.

They chat as they eat, each slice different, but just as good as the other. Trina asks him about the shop and when it was started it; Ryan tells her about their original location, and about how much work it took to get it to this one. He shows her some photos on his phone of the renovations they did.

After that, Trina shows him some pictures of Kiara, her youngest niece, for whom she's attempting to make this cake, and Ryan says she's really is one of the cutest kids he's ever seen.

It's easy, talking to Ryan; perhaps easier than Trina's found it to talk to someone in a while, particularly someone she'll admit that she likes. Trina only finds this instant level of comfort with women; which explains why her last long-term relationship. Her most recent flings have been women and Trina doesn't know if she's ever connected with anyone this instantly before.

The ease makes her wonder if he's too good to be true? Whether, in a moment, the other shoe will drop? However, Ryan's casual mention that he's single causes her stomach to flutter; her body's telling her literally to follow her gut and switch off her brain for a second.

Trina is smiling and blushing like a fool now. Ryan is decent enough not to draw attention to it. She's trying to work out how to let him know that she's single too, and most definitely interested - she can't stop herself from licking her lips. The door opens and Ryan turns to see who's entered, the angle perfectly displaying his chiseled jawline and neck muscles.

"Hey, Mom," says Ryan, and now Trina knows the connection, she can clearly see the resemblance. "Any luck with the strawberries?"

"Yes," his mother says putting several punnets of the ruby red fruit on the counter before wandering over to them at the table. "Ollie's Organics just had a delivery and gave me a deal on the price."

"That's great!" Ryan says, turning back to Trina and raising an eyebrow. "Supply-chain issues," he says and Trina nods.

"Which's your favorite, sweetheart?" Ryan's mother says, with the name 'Sarah' embroidered in orange on her chef's jacket.

"Chocolate," Trina gushes. "Though, I think I'll go for the vanilla this time."

"Yes, vanilla is our most popular for weddings, a real crowd-pleaser," says Sarah.

"Oh, no," she says. "I'm not—"

"When are you getting married, dear? We haven't got a lot of slots left this side of Christmas, I hope this one's told you that?" She nudges Ryan.

Trina glances at Ryan and knows the feeling.

"Sorry. I'm not getting married," Trina says. Sarah pucks her lips. "Well, It's just me."

"Oh," Sarah says. "I—"

"Trina's buying some cake mix for this weekend," Ryan says with his eyes fixed on Trina.

"I see," says Sarah, her eyebrows furrows towards her son. She turns to take the strawberries off the counter. "Ryan, could I speak to you in the kitchen for a minute, please? I need to ask you about the supply of caramel."

Ryan's head whips over resembling that of a kid who's been caught with his hand in the cookie jar. "Sure," he says, slowly, as he rises from the table. "I'll—be right back," he says before slipping through the kitchen door.

Trina fiddles with the napkin in her lap, trying, and failing, not to eavesdrop on what's happening in the kitchen, catching snippets here and there.

"It's not a big deal, Mama!"

"That service is for weddings only, Ryan."

"I'm trying to help her out—Mom."

"That costs $50!"

Trina's eyes widen feeling guilty that she has gotten Ryan into trouble. She looks at her watch; seeing she needs to head back to the office soon. Trina starts to tidy the table, brushing the crumbs into her hand and then onto one of the empty plates, stacking their glasses and refolding the napkins. Ryan and Sarah's voices are still echoing through from the kitchen.

"If this is because of some crush of yours, Mr. Ryan—"

Trina trips over the leg of one of the chairs as she hurries to gather her things, hanging her lanyard back around her neck, nearly ripping an earring out in the process. She's deciding whether she's going to stay or flee when Ryan reappears on the shop floor, red-faced and with his hair mussed up.

"Thanks for letting me taste the cakes," Trina says, wringing her hands.

"No problem," Ryan says, perhaps a little too loudly. "Did you want to buy some cake mix?"

"Yeah, why not. I'll take the vanilla, please." Trina decides she's going to go along, ignoring what just happened.

"Here you are," Ryan says, reaching up to the shelf and grabbing one of the bags. "This should be the right amount for your tin."

Trina is impressed that Ryan remembers what size tin she bought yesterday because she certainly doesn't!

He rings her up on the register. "That'll be $7.50."

"What about the cake frosting?"

"Oh no, that's fine, don't worry." Trina hands over a twenty-dollar bill. She then grabs the bag and hurries towards the door.

"Wait, ma'am!" Ryan calls after her. "You forgot your change."

"Keep it," Trina says stepping over the doormat while heading out.

CHAPTER THREE

Ryan is about to start counting the cash in the register when the bell above the door sounds at 5:25 PM for the second time this week. And, for the third time in as many days, he feels his cheeks start to redden and his pulse quickens as he takes in the woman walking through the door.

Today, Trina's business attire is swapped for a pair of checkered yoga tights with splotches of maroon and pink, a sports bra, and a white vest top. She has her hair up into a bun and is carrying a yoga mat and an Adidas sports bag along with her handbag and laptop bag.

Ryan has to work very hard not to let his mouth drop when he sees she looks stressed.

"Trinnie, hey," Ryan says. "Everything ok?"

"The cake sank."

"Sank?"

"It has this huge dip in the middle." She says. "I think my oven is broken."

"Oh gosh," Ryan says. "Do you need some more cake mix? I can go grab you some on the house."

"No, no, I can't," Trina says, placing her hand on top of his on the counter, to stop him from leaving. It felt like it was to stop Ryan from breathing more like. It takes her a couple of seconds to realize what she's done and she quickly moves it. "I don't have time to make another cake this week, I'm teaching a class tonight and tomorrow. Oh god, when am I going to do this right?"

Ryan tries not to get distracted by the sight of her back and shoulder muscles. He wants to get lost in her, but Ryan does his best to distract her, to find out a little more about this woman who intrigues him so much.

"What are you teaching?"

"Oh, me—" Trina stutters. "Tonight, I'm having a barre class in a studio uptown, then tomorrow is my weekly elderly fitness session I do at a local retirement home."

"In a retirement home?" Ryan says. "That's amazing. Which one?"

"Red Oaks up on Chambry Street."

"You're kidding?" he says.

"Do you know it?"

"Yeah, we donate cakes and pastries to them for their coffee mornings on Wednesdays."

"Sometimes, I went to those as well before class."

"That's crazy?" Ryan says. "That we

both have been there but never met? Do you know Devin?"

Trina chuckles. "Oh yeah. I know Devin!"

She smiles seemingly much calmer now. He watches her reach out to turn the charity tub around so that Trina can read which organization it supports - a local women's shelter.

"And a barre class? Is that a ballet thing?" Ryan asks, intrigued, noticing the definition in Trina's legs and the shape of her bottom. He tries not to stare for too long, but he can't help to do so.

"It's based on ballet, but it's more of a fitness class; strength training, cardio, and flexibility," Trina explains. Ryan nods along. "We use resistance bands and dumbbells, but mostly it's bodyweight stuff. This class has become quite popular in the city now, and the studio I work for is all female-owned, which is pretty cool too."

"That's interesting," Ryan says. "Can men join?"

"Of course!" Trina says. "Why, do you want to come?"

"It sounds like an intense workout." The thought of lifting any weights around Trina sounds appalling. He's spent most of the day frosting three hundred chocolate cupcakes with strawberry buttercream and his hands and wrists are aching.

"For sure," Trina says. "I can't stand the gym. I see you are fit. Do you work out regularly?"

"I rarely have the time so I end up doing stuff in the house and at buddy's place on the weekends." Ryan gestures to the shop around him and Trina nods. "I do pushups in the mornings regularly."

"Oh, me too," Trina smiles.

Ryan nods. "But aside from that, I normally unpack the delivery guy's van three times a week and play a bit of football when I can. My aunt and cousins own a field, so sometimes I'll help out there during the summer."

"Ah, so there's more than one family business you're involved with?"

"Baking and football, that's what us Dales do."

"That's really lovely," Trina says, glancing away. She checks the time on the fitness tracker.

"So I have a solution for your cake woes," Ryan says. "How about I defrost one of our 'emergency cakes' for you to come and collect tomorrow? It's fresh. What do you think?"

"No, I couldn't…" Trina says, but Ryan interrupts her. "It's not a problem. I have plenty in there that I made to restock for the busy season."

"Are you sure?" Trina says. Ryan knows she's being polite and offering him the out, but he declines and nods.

"Thank you," Trina exhales, grabbing his upper arm. "Thank you so much." Then, she leans over the counter to give

Ryan a quick kiss on the cheek. Ryan clears his throat and she pulls away with a shy little smirk.

A car horn outside startles them and Trina blushes before dashing off. Ryan stands behind the register caught up in the moment, already dreading seeing her for perhaps the final time tomorrow.

CHAPTER FOUR

It's been crazy in the shop all day; people coming in placing orders, deliveries, and lots of questions. Ryan hasn't had a moment to sit down, and even had to call in his cousin at lunchtime, alongside with the delivery driver. Despite the frantic nature of the day, it hasn't skipped Ryan's mind that Trina hasn't come in. He's barely had a second to keep an eye out for her, but he's well aware that the cake is still waiting in the fridge for her.

The shop finally quiets down around five o'clock, giving Ryan and his mother a moment to catch their breaths and prep for for the orders coming in tomorrow. With a minute to go until half-past five, Ryan wanders towards the door ready to lock it, mind whirring about how he's going to get the cake to Trina now, when, suddenly, there's the sound of heels clicking on the concrete skids to a halt at the door, looking flustered. Trina startles when she sees Ryan, clearly not expecting him to have his face pressed up against the glass. She smiles as he moves to open the door.

"I'm so sorry—I'm late," Trina says. "My boss stopped by my desk and I couldn't slip away."

"Don't worry," Ryan says, nearly reaching out to put his hand on her arm. "Let me grab your cake, I'll be two seconds."

Ryan darts into the kitchen, completely ignoring his mother's questions as he grabs the box from the fridge. He doesn't know what he's going to say to her and is praying she'll be in too much of a rush to get home to stay behind to interrogate him.

Trina looks nervous as he reappears with the cake, biting at her bottom lip, though she smiles when she sees him.

"Here you go," Ryan says, placing the cake into her arms. Trina looks so uncomfortable, he kind of wants to snatch the cake back and give her a hug instead.

"Hang on," Trina says, looking around for somewhere to put the cake down "I need to pay you."

"No. Please," Ryan raises his hands. "It's on the house."

"But—" Trina starts.

"Please, this is the least I can do to try and make your life easy."

"Are you sure? This is cutting into your profits, Ryan."

"I am more than sure," he says. "It's my pleasure."

"Thank you," she whispers.

"It really is my pleasure," Ryan repeats again, stepping a little closer. Trina too moves forwards and looks up at him through her dark lashes, meeting his eyes and holding his gaze. Several moments pass and neither of them blinks as if they're daring each other to look away. She exhales and bites her lip and he licks his in response.

The sound of Ryan's ringtone – it's his brother calling -interrupts their moment. He curses in his head and mumbles an apology as he answers, though he hardly listens to Grayson as Trina smiles and ducks her head as she turns towards the door. Ryan grabs a business card from next to the register and runs over to her, holding up a finger. Tucking his phone, he takes a pen from his jacket pocket and scrawls his cell number onto it.

Trina's fingers are tentative as she takes the card from him. Ryan covers the microphone. "In case you need help, later? Or, you know, next time you need a cake?" Trina smiles, her cheeks redden.

She mouths 'thank you' and nods as he opens the door for her to exit.

"Ryan? Are you listening to me?" Grayson's voice cuts through the ringing in his ears and, in a bit of a daze, Ryan can continue the conversation - about their cousin's Shawn's upcoming tenth wedding anniversary - whilst he finishes cleaning before he closes the shop.

———

Trina nearly drops her phone when it vibrates just seconds after she texts Ryan late that evening. She thought he'd be asleep, and wishes she hadn't.

"Ryan, I'm so sorry for waking you. I need your help," Trina texted.

"I'm up. Let's talk." Ryan replied back.

"Okay," Trina responds, her fingers slipping so that her phone's autocorrect has to come to her rescue.

The phone's ringtone goes on for a

few seconds, and Trina takes a deep breath.

"Hi," Trina says.

"Hi, Trina. What's up?" Ryan asks so gently that she wants to burst into tears.

"I don't know why I thought I could do this. This cake thing has been a nightmare from the beginning," Trina says.

"Hey, relax," he says. "Now tell me what's happened and I'll see if I can help."

Trina begins telling Ryan about how she started rolling out the fondant, only for her to have not used enough powdered sugar on the surface, so it got stuck. She had rolled it again and used more - she looks around the kitchen and winces at sugar everywhere - but the fondant began tearing and became grainy. Her box of powdered sugar - which has been in her cupboard for far too long - must have dampened.

Ryan hums as Trina explains how she tried to put the powdered sugar on the cake, hoping to disguise it, but then hadn't rolled it out large enough to cover the surface. When she tried to peel it off, she had taken most of the cake away.

"I swear to God, Ryan, I could have dropped it on the floor and it would look better than it does now. It's a total mess." A tear trickles down her face.

"One second." Ryan's quiet for a few seconds and Trina's worried feeling guilty that she's ruined the cake he so kindly gave her. "You still there?"

"I'm here. I'm so sorry," Trina says.

"I'll make another cake for you tomorrow."

"What? No, Ryan, you can't—"

"No, Trina. It's fine, I can put something together in an hour or so."

"I can't let you do that."

"Trina," Ryan says. "What's your job?"

"Oh, why?" Trina was puzzled. "I'm a partner at a law firm."

"Ok," Ryan says. "Wow, that's great."

Trina senses Ryan got a little side-tracked. "So, you wouldn't ask me to negotiate or stand up in court or whatever, would you?"

"No. Why?"

"Because this I can do for you, Trina. We're professionals and know how important it is to be on time?"

"If you say so but this—"

"Trina, I want to do this for you."

"Oh—well, if you say so," she says. "I guess I can't convince you otherwise."

"There's just one favor I need to ask of you," Ryan says.

"Okay, whatever."

"Don't tell my mother." Trina attempts to smother her chuckle with a cough. "I know, I know, I'm thirty-two and co-owner of the shop, but she'll kill me if she finds out I've been in there after closing!"

"No, Ryan, you can't do this. It's going to cause a problem between you and your mother. Really, I can go to buy one at the supermarket and get some cup-cakes to go along with it."

"Those are not fresh, and probably been sitting there for over a week!" Ryan says. "If it would make you feel better, why don't you come and help me?"

Trina pauses for a moment. Then sur-prises herself by saying she really wouldn't mind.

"Ok, I'll see you tomorrow?"

In Trina's mind, she pictures him stuffing his hands in his pockets. "Yeah, I'll be there," Trina says. "How's 5:25? I'll be off around then."

"Sounds great," Ryan says. "Bye, Trinnie."

"Bye," Trina replies.

Trina dumps the fondant in the trash, laughing as she cleans up the mess she managed to make.

CHAPTER FIVE

Ryan hurried his mother out of the back of the shop and into her car when the bell chimes. "I'll make sure everything is ready for tomorrow. We have a delivery I need to check on before closing."

"Ok and make sure you check the temperatures on the refrigerators before you leave."

"Yes, Mom."

Sarah pulls off and Ryan dashes back inside to the kitchen and onto the shop floor, smiling when he sees Trina waiting at the door. Her laptop bag in one hand

and a small Adidas sports bag in the other. Her hair is now in a ponytail.

"Hi Trina," Ryan says, trying to remain cool and collected. "Come on back." He cocks his head towards the doorway and Trina nods following him into the kitchen.

———

Stainless-steel benches shine brightly under the strip lights, as do the fronts of the industrial-sized ovens and the row of mixers. To the right, are racks housing every size of cake tin from two-inch dessert rings to 20" squares.

Ryan pulls out a plastic stool from under the island in the middle. The thick marble countertop is cool to the touch and perfect for chocolate and pastry work. Ryan watches enchanted as Trina glides her hand over the polished stone, her finger tracing one of his favorite swirls in the right-hand corner.

Ryan passes Trina an orange apron then instructs her about making the cake leveled, filled, stacked and crumb coated. He answers her questions about flavors and techniques, about where he trained and why.

Trina sneaks a taste of everything Ryan has put into the cake; the raspberry coulis he swirls into the buttercream spread between each layer. Each is faintly flavored with grated lemon zest to bring out the zing in the raspberries that Ryan pulls apart and studs into the pink and white milky way adorning the champagne-colored sponge.

He pinches off a small ball of fondant from the kilogram block he's kneading, making it pliable through the heat of his hands, and gives it to Trina to taste as well. Trina's delighted as she chews on the taster; Ryan's fondant has never had a complaint. Ryan then adds a faint drop of lemon extract to the dough, to offset the sweetness and complement the cake he has so stacked and kneads the fondant further to fully bring out the flavor.

Ryan then dusts the end strip of the marble counter with a small layer of cornstarch - when she asks why he uses it instead of powdered sugar he explains how it's easier to dust off the excess and doesn't dry out the fondant nor mess with the flavor balance. He begins to roll out the fondant, turning the disk between each roll so that it doesn't stick, ensuring an even thickness throughout, and ending with a near-perfect circle ready to be transferred onto the cake.

"Shall we put her name on the cake?" Ryan asks afterward, wandering towards the shelf with the bins filled with cutters and molds.

"Yeah, that would be great," says Trina, moving to join him. He grabs the tin of alphabet cutters and notices that she is reaching up on her tiptoes to get the bin labeled 'Flowers and Butterflies'. He stretches over her to get it.

"And do you want me to make a little animal or something to go on top? To give it a little more dimension and height?"

"That sounds good," Trina says. "Do you have time for that?"

Ryan glances over to the clock - black metal with the numbers and 'Miller' cut out of it - and sees that it's only a quarter past six. "Yeah, I have time. What animal do you think she'd like?"

"Well, Henry and Luna have had a bit of a thing with elephants, so maybe one of those?"

"Great, I love making elephants!" He moves over to the other shelves with the fondant and modeling paste. "So we'll need grey for the elephant. How about this light blue and this egg yolk yellow for the letters and details? We should put some flowers and butterflies around the edge."

"That sounds perfect," Trina says.

"They've tried not to be overly pink and girly with her so I know they'll love that."

"I totally get that. I swear, I cringe every time someone comes in and wants to order a gender reveal cake." Ryan rubs at the back of his neck, "I mean, people are perfectly entitled to do whatever they like, but boy equals blue and girl equals pink is so stereotypical before a kid is even born."

"I agree."

They make their way back to the counter and Ryan sets Trina up rolling out some smaller pieces of the colored fondant between two bits of dowel to ensure even thickness and teaches her the easiest way to use the plunger cutters to get clean edges on the letters, butterflies, and daisies. He sets to work on the elephant, stopping as quiet curses and grunts come from Trina, whose talents very clearly lie elsewhere.

"You doing okay there?"

"I really am useless at this," says

Trina, dropping the cutter back onto the counter and squishing the droopy daisy back into a small ball.

"Here," Ryan steps over and sets her up with a new piece of fondant that hasn't been overworked to the point of cracking. "You need to keep it moving so it doesn't stick to the surface." He holds the rolling pin out, but she hesitates in taking it.

"Show me," Trina says smiling. Ryan knows she's flirting, and he goes with it, stepping closer and slightly to the side so he's right behind her. He reaches his arms around hers and Trina takes the rolling pin, but he holds on too, whispering instructions into her ear. Ryan sees her head tilted slightly to the side. His lips are close to her neck and she smells so good that he just wants to latch on there.

Then, Trina's phone rings at the other end of the counter causing them to back away from each other. They have been moving the rolling pin back and forth for a few moments without it having any effect, and the fondant was already at the right thickness. Ryan steps back as she moves from the circle, and Trina tucks a strand of hair behind her ear as she reaches for her phone. But then she pauses, her hand still outstretched, and her mouth drops when she sees the cake.

"Oh my god, this is amazing!" Trina says, delighted, turning back to him.

"Thanks," Ryan says, rubbing at the back of his neck and smiling as he watches her lean down to inspect the paste elephant more closely, her hands quivering as if eager to touch it but knowing she shouldn't. Trina smiles as she checks her phone and then comes back over and they continue their lesson in cutting out the letters and shapes, though the tension has dissipated a little.

———

Twenty minutes later, the cake is finished and they take a step back to survey their work. Trina claps and does a little jump for joy. "This is gorgeous, Ryan, thank you so much!" Before he can brush off her compliment, Trina throws her arms around him, which she pulls away from before he has a chance to savor it. He moves the cake to the turntable on the side bench and Trina follows him, pulling her phone from her pocket, then begins to snap photos of it.

Whilst Trina does this, Ryan sets to work cleaning up the slab, brushing off the corn starch from the counter before filling a bucket that once held a kilo of green dragées with warm soapy water, and wiping it down before drying it off. Once it's dry, Ryan cleans it once more, crouching down so the counter is at eye level and he can inspect for any signs that he was here after his mother cleaned it a couple of hours ago. Once he's done, he throws his apron into the pile of laundry in the corner by his backpack.

Ryan passes Trina the box and she

slides the cake into it as he stacks up the items they've used and put them back. The punnet of raspberries tips over as he opens the fridge, the ruby jewels tumbling silently to the floor. He puts the container of frosting and the rind-less lemons onto the nearest shelf before shutting the door and bending down to pick them up. Once Ryan's down on his knees, he finds himself face to face with Trina, who is already picking up the berries.

"You don't have to," Ryan says, as he scoops a couple, his fingertips are smeared.

"It's fine, don't worry about it," she says, as she reaches for one that rolled a little further away. Ryan watches Trina from the corner of his eye, marveling at how beautiful she looks, with that orange apron on.

Trina hisses suddenly and stands, dropping several of the raspberries as she grabs her calf. Ryan reaches out for her, his hand steadying her leg, her free one coming to rest on his shoulder for support.

"Sorry," she grits out. "Cramps." She rubs her calf, leaving streaks of juice across her skin.

"It'll be okay," Ryan says, aware of how close to her he's kneeling, his hand on the back of her knee.

Trina feels it twitch because suddenly her eyes are on his and she's looking down at him. At first, she seems surprised, and Ryan gulps. But then her gaze becomes charged by something else entirely. Without thinking, Ryan comes upwards and presses his mouth to hers.

Trina's lips taste like raspberries and sugar, a flavor so familiar to him. Ryan runs his tongue along the seam of her lips, their tongues tangling, sighing into the kiss as their hands begin to wander and they shuffle closer together. Their bodies are radiating heat despite the cool temperature inside.

Ryan tugs the tie at the back of Trina's apron and once it's undone, it falls, breaking their kiss for the briefest time to remove it. She huffs before recapturing his lips again.

He creeps his hands towards her buttocks and sinks his fingertips into the flesh, marveling at her impressive muscles squeezing at its firmness.

Trina sighs and she presses closer, one hand running up into his hair as the other fists the front of his chef's jacket. For once the heavy cotton that's so comfortable to wear, feels hot.

"Take it off," Ryan husks out, pulling away from her and pulling open the popper fastening at the neck. Trina's eyes raise and her mouth twitches. Trina darts forwards like a cat swiping at its prey and rips open the rest of the poppers, leaving his jacket hanging open and revealing the sleeveless black shirt he wears beneath. She pulls at that too and he steps forward to reach for her again, their hands roaming contrasting paths across the other's body; hers under his shirt and up across his abs, his traveling down from her waist to the hem of her skirt.

Their lips meet again, almost feral now as they devour each other; more teeth than caressing tongues. Ryan starts to walk them back towards the counter, hands moving further up and under her skirt until they're on her ass again, which is barely covered by her lacy panties that he'd quite like to rip off now. He moves his index finger lightly across her center, Trina's breathing hitches and she lets out a gasp. "Ohhh, oh!" The sound makes Ryan's erection nearly pierce his boxers open.

Trina pants as Ryan lifts her up on the counter. She encircles her legs around him, her mouth opens feeling his erection at her center against her. She grips his hair tighter, her fingers scratch his scalp most seductively and Ryan nearly comes.

"Do you know that I fell in love with you the moment you walked in?"

The second the words fell from his lips, Ryan was worried he'd said the wrong thing. Trina smiles. "I did too. Now hurry and fuck me before your mother comes," Trina says.

Ryan giggles as they pull off their clothes and get into position.

ACKNOWLEDGMENTS

Thanks for reading and please leave a review. This will really help us out.

Consider joining our mailing list by sending us a hi at therealjustbae@gmail.com. We give out FREE Audiobook codes all the time.

Join our IG page here: instagram.com/justbaebooks

Join our FB page here: facebook.com/authorjustbae

Best of regards,
Just Bae

A Nurse Got Me: Zoe

A Desi Got Me: Raj

A Deewana Got Me: Katrina

My Big Daddy Got Me: Dominic

A Policeman Got Me: Al